Quentin Blake

MISTER MAGNOLIA

RED FOX

RED FOX
UK | USA | Canada | Ireland | Australia
India | New Zealand | South Africa

Red Fox is part of the Penguin Random House group of companies
whose addresses can be found at global.penguinrandomhouse.com.

www.penguin.co.uk   www.puffin.co.uk   www.ladybird.co.uk

 Penguin
Random House
UK

First published by Jonathan Cape 1980
Red Fox edition published 1999
This edition published 2018
001

Made and printed in China
A CIP catalogue record for this book is available from the British Library

ISBN: 978–1–782–95860–4

All correspondence to:
Red Fox, Penguin Random House Children's
80 Strand, London WC2R 0RL

Mr Magnolia has only one boot.

He has an old trumpet
that goes rooty-toot –

And two lovely sisters
who play on the flute –

But Mr Magnolia has only one boot.

In his pond live a frog
        and a toad and a newt –

He has green parakeets
who pick holes in his suit –

And some very fat owls
who are learning to hoot –
But Mr Magnolia
has only one boot.

He gives rides to his friends
when he goes for a scoot –

And the splash is immense
        when he comes down
            the chute –

But Mr Magnolia
    has only one boot.

Just look at the way that
he juggles with fruit!

The mice all march past
as he takes the salute!

And his dinosaur!
What a MAGNIFICENT
brute!

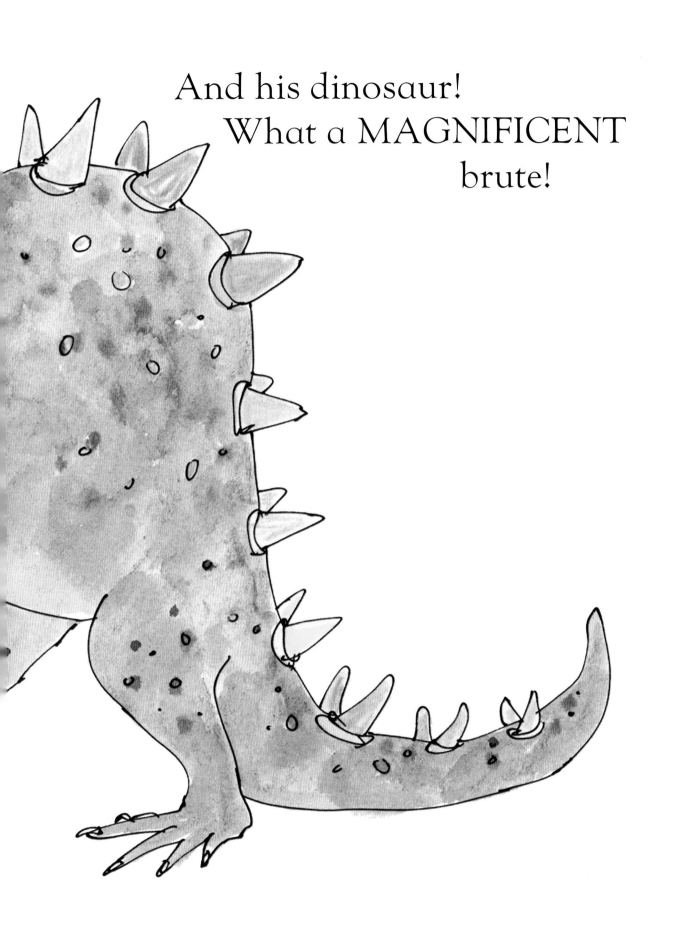

But Mr Magnolia –
poor Mr Magnolia!
– Mr Magnolia
has
only one boot . . .

Hey –

Wait a minute . . .

Now then . . .

Keep going . . .

What's this?

Look!

It's a boot!
It's a boot!

Whoopee
for Mr Magnolia's
new boot!

Good night.